A Note from the Author

I am thrilled that *Where's My Teddy?* has remained in print long enough to have the honor of a twenty-fifth anniversary edition. I have always been delighted when children tell me it is their favorite story, and now I am just as likely to hear the same from parents who grew up reading it.

Where's My Teddy? sprang out of my love of playing with words and rhymes. It's a childish pleasure, and perhaps that's one reason children enjoy this story—in which Eddie's teddy is, of course, named Freddie. What else?

Behind the wordplay, the book explores the subject of fear, especially in relation to being small. It's an important topic if you are four and the world around you is very big and populated by giants called grown-ups. Although Eddie is scared by the great big bear, he discovers that the bear is scared, too, and that he needs his teddy just as much as Eddie needs Freddie. By the end of the book, Eddie's heart may be racing, but he has learned that the world is not such a scary place after all. I think the same goes for the bear, and maybe for the reader, too.

Jez Alborough

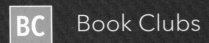

BC Book Clubs

Title	*Where's My Teddy?*
Grade	Kindergarten
Author/ Illustrator	Jez Alborough
Genre	Fiction
Text Set 7	Understanding Feelings

Begin numbering this book on the left-hand page with body text beginning: "Eddie's off to find his teddy."

Book Talk

Do you have a special blanket or stuffed animal? This book is about a boy named Eddie who loses his very special teddy bear. When he goes into the woods to find teddy, he finds a giant teddy and a giant real bear! Will Eddie find his perfect little teddy? What will the giant bear do? You might be surprised to find out how much these two have in common!

Summary

A boy named Eddie has lost his teddy bear and goes off into the woods to find it. He notices a giant teddy who is too big to cuddle. Then he runs into a giant bear and realizes that the giant teddy belongs to the real bear who is holding Eddie's tiny teddy. The giant bear and Eddie each get their own teddy back and run through the dark woods back to their homes as fast as they could.

Messages

A comfort object can make you feel safe and protected. Everyone feels afraid sometimes.

Important Text Characteristics

- Themes that are familiar to children (comfort objects, safety, fear, home)
- Colorful illustrations that convey character's feelings
- Large font and all caps used for emphasis in the text
- Rhyme and repetition add to the rhythm of the story

Goals

Refer to *The Fountas & Pinnell Literacy Continuum* for Grade K and choose appropriate goals. Consider these:

Listening and Speaking

- Look at the speaker when spoken to
- Take turns when speaking

Building Deep Understanding

- Infer that even though Eddie and the bear are different from each other, they are have feelings in common (being afraid, feeling safe)

- Notice the writer's use of playful language (rhyme, rhythm)

Writing About Reading

- Draw and write about connections between the ideas in the book and children's own life experience

Prepare for the Discussion

Tell children when you will be meeting. *To prepare for our book club, read or listen to the book and think what you want to say about it. Use a sticky note to mark one or two pages that you want to talk about.*

Discuss the Book

Invite children to share parts of the book they want to talk about. Remind them to look at the speaker when spoken to and take turns when speaking. If needed, select from the following prompts to support thinking and talking.

Facilitating the Discussion	Suggested Prompts
Eddie's bear must be very special to him. Do you think the bear's teddy is just as special?	▶ Who has something to share? ▶ Talk more about that.
Let's look at pages 5 and 6. Eddie hasn't seen anything scary yet, but he tiptoes and looks afraid. Why do you think he does that?	▶ What do you think? ▶ Does anyone want to add to that?
What might happen if Eddie and the giant bear each kept the teddies that didn't belong to them?	▶ What makes you think that? ▶ Did anyone else wonder about something?
Talk about how the illustrations and the words show how characters feel.	▶ Can you find an example that shows what you mean?
Eddie is afraid of the "scary" forest at the beginning of the story. The bear lives in the forest, so why do you think the bear is afraid?	▶ Why do you think that? ▶ What do others think about that?
Have you ever felt afraid like Eddie does in this story? What makes you feel safe?	▶ What does this story remind you of?

Evaluate the Discussion

Refer to the goals. Invite children to self-evaluate how well they took turns speaking, as well as their participation and contribution to helping one another building understanding of the book.

Extend the Discussion: Write About Reading

Draw a picture that shows one part of the book when Eddie and the bear both felt afraid. Then draw a picture of a time when you have felt afraid.

For my dearest Rikka

25th U.S. anniversary edition 2017
First published in Great Britain in 1992 by Walker Books Ltd., London.

The Library of Congress has cataloged the original hardcover edition as follows:

Alborough, Jez.
Where's my teddy? / Jez Alborough.
Summary: When a small boy named Eddie goes searching
for his lost teddy in the dark woods, he comes across a gigantic
bear with a similar problem.
ISBN 978-1-56402-048-2 (hardcover)
[1. Teddy bears — Fiction. 2. Bears — Fiction.
3. Stories in rhyme.] I. Title.
PZ8.3.A24Wh 1992
[E] — dc20   91-58765

ISBN 978-1-56402-280-6 (paperback)
ISBN 978-0-7636-9816-4 (twenty-fifth anniversary hardcover)
ISBN 978-0-7636-9871-3 (twenty-fifth anniversary paperback)

17 18 19 20 21 22 APS 10 9 8 7 6 5 4 3 2 1

Printed in Humen, Dongguan, China

This book was typeset in Garamond.
The illustrations were done in watercolor, crayon, and pencil.

Candlewick Press
99 Dover Street
Somerville, Massachusetts 02144

visit us at www.candlewick.com

WHERE'S MY TEDDY?

JEZ ALBOROUGH

CANDLEWICK PRESS

Eddie's off to find his teddy.
Eddie's teddy's name is Freddie.

He lost him in the woods somewhere.
It's dark and horrible in there.

"Help!" said Eddie. "I'm scared already!
I want my bed! I want my teddy!"

He tiptoed
on and on
until . . .

something
made him stop
quite still.

Look out! he thought. There's something there!

WHAT'S THAT?

"You're too big to huddle and cuddle," he said,

"and I'll never fit both of us into my bed."

Then out of the darkness,
clearer and clearer,
the sound of a sobbing
came nearer and nearer.

Soon the whole woods
could hear the voice bawl,
"How did you get to be
tiny and small?
You're too small to
huddle and cuddle," it said,
"and you'll only get lost
in my giant-sized bed!"

It was a gigantic bear
and a tiny teddy
stomping toward . . .

the giant teddy and Eddie.

"MY TED!"
gasped the bear.
"A BEAR!"
screamed Eddie.

"A BOY!"
yelled the bear.
"MY TEDDY!"
cried Eddie.

Then they ran and they ran
through the dark woods
back to their homes
as fast as they could . . .

all the way back
to their snuggly beds,
where they huddled
and cuddled their
own little teds.